Shamoo

A Whale of a Cow

BY Ros Hill

Distributed by Publishers Group West

Most cows spend their lives in a pasture, happily chewing on grass. But not Shamoo...

Shamoo loved to swim. He loved the backstroke and freestyle. He loved how peaceful it felt to float on his back and look up at the sky.

Yet as much as he enjoyed his little pond,
Shamoo yearned for something more.
Something big. Something different.
Something like the sea.

One day while Shamoo was staring at the sea, a rail on the fence broke loose. Without a doubt, Shamoo knew it was time to explore the ocean.

Shamoo paddled through the gentle waves. The water was so deep and tasted salty on his tongue. With the birds above and the fish below, Shamoo didn't notice that he was swimming farther and farther out to sea.

And then, from out of the deep blue, a gigantic wave emerged, towering over Shamoo.

The wave crashed down, trapping Shamoo underwater, and a riptide swept him along. He struggled against it, but the pull was just too powerful. He held his breath tightly, hoping the current would weaken.

Shamoo finally broke free. Gasping for air, he looked all around and could not see his familiar pasture or the other cows anywhere. He began mooing for help.

From the depths, it rose.

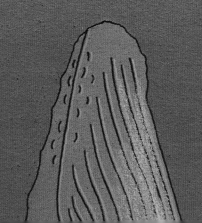

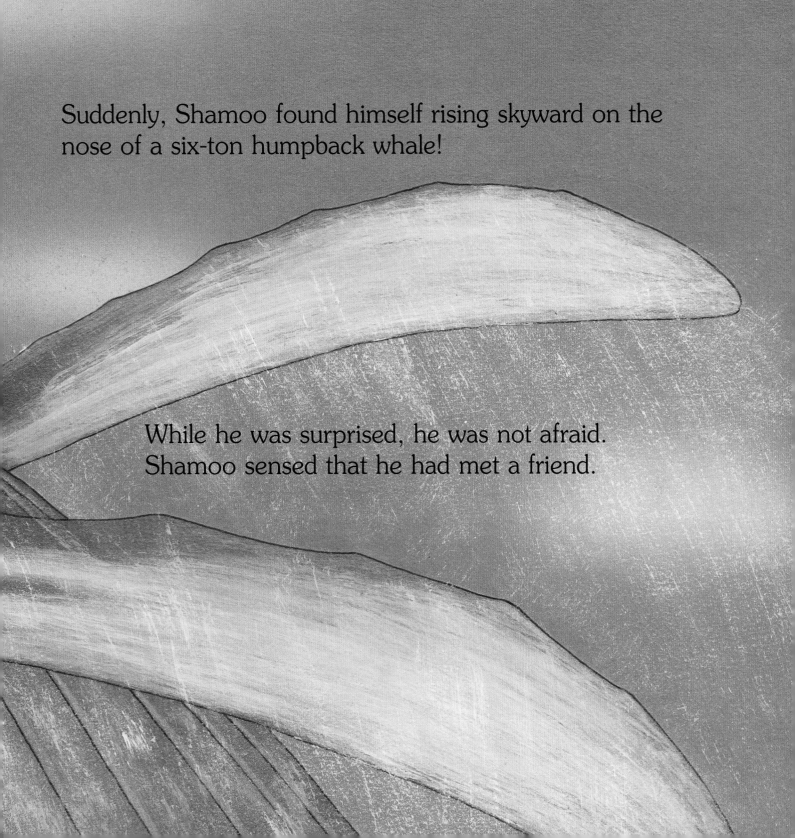

Suddenly, Shamoo found himself rising skyward on the nose of a six-ton humpback whale!

While he was surprised, he was not afraid. Shamoo sensed that he had met a friend.

Her name was Baleen and she turned out to be a friend and a teacher. First, she taught Shamoo how to swim underwater.

Shamoo learned how to breach.

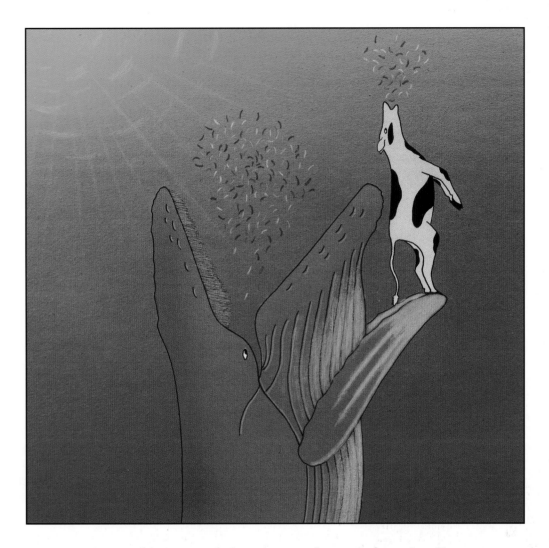

He learned how to hunt for krill.

And, most importantly, Baleen taught him how to avoid predators.

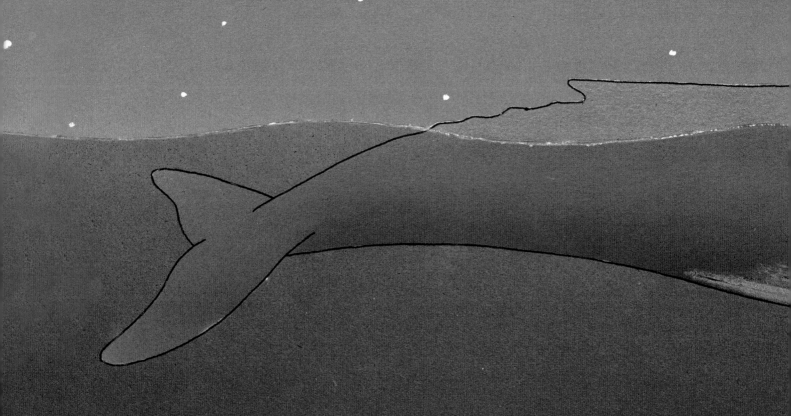

That night, Shamoo lay down on his six-ton friend and looked up at a sky filled with thousands of stars. He was thrilled with all he'd learned. But to his surprise, he felt a bit lonely. He started to think about his pasture, the tasty crunch of fresh grass, and his old friends.

In the morning, Shamoo told Baleen what he was feeling. She understood and agreed to take him home.

Shamoo was glad to feel solid ground under his hooves again. "Goodbye!" he called to the whale. "We'll meet again!"

Back in the pasture, Shamoo was determined to teach the other cows how to swim. Maybe, one day, they too could experience the thrill of the open sea.

And one day, they did.

To my wife, Vikki, for her critical (but helpful) eyes, and to my kids: Brookney, Brandon, and Bailey, whose summer days at the pool would never have been complete without my "Shamoo!" splashes.
-RH

Shamoo: A Whale of a Cow
Copyright © 2005 Ros Hill
A publication of
Milk and Cookies Press,
a division of ibooks, inc.
Distributed by Publishers Group West
1700 Fourth Street, Berkeley, CA 94710
ibooks, inc.
24 West 25th Street, 11th floor, New York, NY 10010
The ibooks, inc. World Wide Web Site address is: http://www.ibooks.net
ISBN: 1-59687-188-1
First ibooks, inc. printing: October 2005
10 9 8 7 6 5 4 3 2 1
Editor - Dinah Dunn
Associate Editor - Robin Bader
Library of Congress Cataloging-in-Publication Data available

Manufactured in China